D0617248

The Amazing Magic Show

The Amazing Magic Show

by P.J. Petersen

Illustrated by
Renée Williams-Andriani

SIMON & SCHUSTER BOOKS FOR YOUNG READERS
Published by Simon & Schuster
New York London Toronto Sydney Tokyo Singapore

SIMON & SCHUSTER BOOKS FOR YOUNG READERS
1230 Avenue of the Americas, New York, New York 10020
Text copyright © 1994 by P.J. Petersen
Illustrations © 1994 by Renée Williams-Andriani
Book design by David Neuhaus.
The text for this book is set in 17-point Sabon.
The illustrations were done in watercolor and ink.
Manufactured in the United States of America.

10 9 8 7 6 5 4 3 2 1

Library of Congress Cataloging-in-Publication Data
Petersen, P.J. The amazing magic show / by P.J. Petersen ;
illustrated by Renée Williams-Andriani.   p. cm.
Summary: After attending a magic show and learning some
tricks, Hal finds a way to get the best of his overbearing older
brother. [1. Brothers—Fiction. 2. Magic tricks—Fiction.]
I. Williams-Andriani, Renée, ill. II. Title.
PZ7.P44197Am 1994 [Fic]—dc20 93-34861 CIP AC
ISBN: 0-671-86581-1

For Karen and Adam Harvey
—P.J.P.

For Vince
—R.W.-A.

Part One:
The Amazing Chuck

Chapter 1

"A magic show!" Hal shouted. "A magic show with The Amazing Victor!" He ran up the front walk.

His big brother, Chuck, grabbed him. "Wait a minute," Chuck said. "We need a plan. We can't just go in and ask Mom and Dad for money."

Hal pulled away from Chuck. "Why not?"

"They might say no. They think we throw our money away."

"I don't throw my money away,"

Hal said. "I give it to the man in the ice cream truck."

Chuck gave Hal a shove. "I'll think of something."

"Let's just ask," Hal said. But he knew Chuck would get his way.

"I've got it," Chuck said. "We'll act so excited they won't even think about money. You jump up and down and say, 'Goody-goody.' I'll do the talking."

"I don't want to say 'Goody-goody,'" Hal said. "It sounds dumb."

"Say it," Chuck told him. "And don't say anything else."

"I don't think this is going to work," Hal said.

Chuck dashed up the steps. "Come on!"

They ran into the kitchen. "Dad, Mom!" Chuck yelled. "Guess what!"

Hal jumped up and down. "Goody-goody," he said. It sounded dumb.

"What is it?" Mom asked.

Dad set down his sandwich. "Do I get three guesses?"

Hal knew the look on Dad's face. "Just tell him," he said to Chuck.

Dad kept right on. "Guess one: You cleaned your room. Guess two: You decided never to watch TV again." He smiled at them. "Am I close?"

"Come on, Dad," Chuck said.

"Guess three: You need some money."

Hal quit jumping up and down. It was all over.

But Chuck turned to Mom. "Rick's dad is taking him to a magic show. A neat one with The Amazing Victor. Rick says we can go with them."

"It'll be fun," Hal said. He looked at Chuck and started jumping again. "Goody-goody."

"How much—" Dad began.

Hal opened his mouth. But Chuck kept talking. "And I love magic. Remember those magic books I used to read?"

"Please," Hal called out. "Please."

"It sounds like fun," Mom said. She looked at Dad.

"How much does the magic show cost?" Dad asked.

Hal knew that Dad wanted an

answer. But Chuck said, "Hal's never seen a real magic show."

Dad looked right at Hal. "How much?"

"Only three dollars," Hal said. Chuck gave him a dirty look.

Dad smiled at Hal. "Only three dollars? You have that much, don't you?"

Hal shook his head. Dad knew he was broke. In fact, he owed Dad a lot of money. He wasn't sure how much.

Dad looked at Chuck. "Do you have three dollars?"

"It'll be a great magic show," Chuck said.

"Hal owes me eight dollars," Dad said. "And Chuck owes me thirteen."

"And they both owe me money," Mom added.

Things looked bad. Hal wondered why Chuck was still smiling.

Dad went on. "Yesterday I got a ride to work. My sons were going to wash my car. For five dollars. And what did I find when I got home?"

"Tommy came over to play," Hal said. "I had to play with him."

"When I got home, the car had mud all over it," Dad said.

"That was an accident," Hal said. "Tommy and I were making mud castles."

"We'll wash it today," Chuck said.

"I took the car to the car wash last night," Dad said.

Uh-oh, thought Hal.

Chuck looked at Mom. "We don't get many chances to go to a magic show. It's only here for one night."

"Don't look so sad," Dad said to Hal. "You can go to the magic show."

"Hooray!" Hal yelled. "Goody-goody." He ran toward the door.

"Wait a minute!" Dad shouted. "I'm not finished."

"Oh." Hal looked back at Dad.

"You can go to the magic show," Dad said. "But you have to earn the money."

Chuck groaned. "How?"

"The lawn is full of weeds," Dad said. "If you dig weeds for an hour, I'll give you the money."

"Weeds?" Hal said.

"It'll be like a magic show," Dad told him. "Amazing Chuck and Amazing

Hal can make the weeds disappear."

Hal started for the door. "Let's go do it," he said.

Chuck grabbed Hal's arm. "Wait a minute."

Hal pulled his arm free.

Chuck looked back at Dad. "We can go if we earn the money, right?"

"That's right," Dad said.

"No problem then," Chuck said. He walked out the door.

Hal followed Chuck. "Are we going to dig weeds now?" he asked.

"No," Chuck said. "Not now. Not ever. That's too much work. And it's too hot. And weeds make you itch. I've got better ideas."

"Good," Hal said. "I hate to weed."

"Remember the deal," Dad called through the door. "If you don't earn the money, you don't go to the magic show."

"No problem," Chuck said.

"Yeah," Hal said. "No problem." He looked at Chuck. "Are you sure there's no problem?"

"You're talking to The Amazing Chuck," Chuck said. "The money will roll in like magic."

Chapter 2

Hal followed Chuck down the front steps. "What do we do?" Hal asked.

"We knock on doors," Chuck said. "We tell people we need money for a magic show. Then we ask if they have work for us."

"We're going to work?" Hal said.

"A little," Chuck said.

Hal shook his head. "Then why not work right here?"

"It's better to work for other people," Chuck said. "You don't have to work so hard. And they pay you more. It'll be easy."

It didn't sound so easy to Hal. "We just knock on doors? Any old doors?"

"No," Chuck said. "We know lots of people around here. We'll ask people we know."

"Oh." Hal felt a little better. But not much.

He looked at their lawn. It was full of weeds. He had never noticed them before. "We could pull weeds for Dad. We could get the radio and listen to music."

"You can pull weeds," Chuck said. "You can get all dirty. And itchy. And tired. The Amazing Chuck has better ideas." He started down the sidewalk.

Hal thought for a minute. Then he ran after Chuck. "I'll go with you."

Chuck went next door to Mrs. Brown's house. Hal stayed right behind him. Chuck told Hal to ring the bell.

"What do I say?" Hal asked.

"Ask her if she has any jobs for us."

Hal backed away from the door. "You do it."

Chuck pushed the doorbell. Then he shoved Hal toward the door. "You ask her. Little guys get more jobs. People feel sorry for them."

"I'm not so little," Hal said.

Mrs. Brown opened the door. Hal couldn't think of what to say. "Look who's here," Mrs. Brown said. "Come on in."

"Hi," Hal said. He started to go inside.

Chuck grabbed his arm. "Go ahead and ask her."

"Would you boys like some oatmeal raisin cookies?" Mrs. Brown asked. "Or is it too soon after lunch?"

"I don't think it's too soon," Hal said.

"Come on into the kitchen," Mrs. Brown said. "I have some just out of the oven."

Hal followed her. Chuck poked him in the back. "Ask her."

"In a minute," Hal said.

Mrs. Brown had them sit at the kitchen table. She brought them each a plate of cookies. "Would you boys like some milk?"

"Yes, please," Hal said. Then he said, "Ouch." Chuck was kicking him under the table.

So Hal said, "Mrs. Brown, do you have some work for us to do?"

Mrs. Brown smiled. "Isn't that nice. You like to help." She looked around the kitchen. "Maybe you could take out the garbage for me. That would be a help. But finish your cookies first."

Hal ate his cookies. Then he took out the garbage.

"You boys are so sweet," said Mrs. Brown. "Come by and see me again sometime."

Back on the street, Chuck gave Hal a push. "Nice going."

"It wasn't my fault," Hal said. "I did what you told me."

"You did not," Chuck said. "I told you to say we needed money for the magic show."

"It's hard to talk about money," Hal said.

"I'll tell you the words to say," Chuck said.

"It's your turn this time."

"Little kids have a better chance."

Chuck made Hal stand outside the Taylors' house until Hal had his speech ready. "Say it one more time," Chuck said. "And smile. Try to look cute. Cute kids get money."

"Hi," Hal said. "We're trying to make money so we can go to a magic show. Do you have any jobs we can do?"

"Okay," Chuck said. "Ring the bell before you forget. And keep smiling."

Hal pushed the doorbell. He heard the Taylors' dog bark. Hal didn't like that dog. It was bigger than he was. It always jumped on him and licked his face. And knocked him down. He heard the dog scratching on the other side of the door. "Nobody's home," he said. He was glad. The dog had made him forget his speech.

Hal heard the music of the ice cream truck. "It's the ice cream man," he yelled.

"Forget it," Chuck said.

"I guess we better not ask Dad for money," Hal said.

"Right," Chuck said. "But if we

make a lot of money, we can go to the magic show *and* buy ice cream."

Hal ran down the street. "Let's hurry."

Nobody was home at the next house. Or the next one. At the Bakers' house, Hal rang the bell and stepped back.

Mrs. Baker yanked open the door. She had her baby in one arm. Her little boy, Brandon, was holding onto her leg. The baby was crying. Hal thought Brandon might start crying any minute. "Yes?" Mrs. Baker said.

"We're looking for work," Hal said. "We want to go to a magic show."

Mrs. Baker didn't seem to hear him. Hal wasn't surprised. The baby was very loud. "Who are you looking for?" she asked.

"We're looking for work," Hal said. "We're doing jobs for people."

"Oh," Mrs. Baker said. "Maybe you could play with Brandon for a few minutes."

"Sure," Hal said.

"Brandon," Mrs. Baker said, "wouldn't you like to go outside and play with the boys?"

"Noooo," Brandon screamed.

"Come on, Brandon," Hal said. "Let's play hide-and-go-seek."

"No!" Brandon shouted. He wrapped his arms around his mother's legs. He stuck out his tongue at Hal. Then he let out a yowl.

"Maybe later," Mrs. Baker said. She closed the door.

"Too bad," Chuck said.

"I think I'd rather pull weeds," Hal said.

Chapter 3

Mr. Finch came to the door with his cat, George, on his shoulder. "We're earning money to go to a magic show," Hal said. "Do you have any jobs for us?"

Mr. Finch smiled. "I sure do, boys."

Hal felt like jumping up and down and saying, "Goody-goody."

"Just look at my lawn," Mr. Finch said. "It's full of weeds. And I can't bend over to pull them."

Hal looked at Mr. Finch's lawn. Then he looked at Chuck.

"Did you hear that?" Chuck said.

"Hear what?" Hal asked.

"Mom's calling us."

Hal listened. "I don't hear anything."

"It's Mom," Chuck said. "And she sounds mad."

Hal still didn't hear anything.

"Come on," Chuck shouted. He raced down the street.

"Good-bye, Mr. Finch," Hal said. He ran after Chuck.

Hal caught up with Chuck at the corner. "Did Mom really call?"

Chuck shook his head. "We had to get out of there. We don't want to pull weeds."

Hal laughed. "Good idea." But then he looked at Chuck. "How are we going to get six dollars?"

"Just leave it to The Amazing Chuck," Chuck said. "We have lots of time."

Hal saw Mrs. Walker in her garage. She was moving boxes.

"Here's our chance," Chuck said. "Be sure to smile and look cute."

"I don't want to look cute," Hal said.

"Cute kids get the money." Chuck gave him a push. "Cute kids go to magic shows."

Hal walked up the driveway. He didn't know if he looked cute. He wasn't sure how to do it.

"Hi, Mrs. Walker," he said. "We're doing jobs to get money for a magic show. Do you have any jobs?" He smiled. He hoped it was a cute smile.

"You can help me haul this stuff to the curb," Mrs. Walker said. "The trash man will be here soon."

"I told you we'd get a job," Chuck said.

Mrs. Walker handed Hal a box. It was full of neat things. Hal was surprised they were for the trash man. "You're throwing these things away?" he asked.

"Yes," Mrs. Walker said. "It's all junk."

Hal looked into the box. "What about this dog collar?"

"It's too small for our dog now," she said.

"Can I have it?"

"Do you have a dog?" she asked.

"No," Hal said. "But I might get one some day." He put the collar in his pocket and carried the box to the curb.

In the next box he found a model plane with part of a wing missing. He also found a yo-yo with no string and a bicycle tire.

"You were a lot of help," Mrs. Walker told them when they were finished. "There's just one more thing. A toy elephant. It's by the front door."

Hal and Chuck ran to get it.

The elephant was pink. And it was almost as tall as Hal. "Look at this thing," Chuck said. "It must have cost a hundred dollars."

"It's kind of dirty," Hal said.

"We could sell it easy," Chuck said.

The elephant had a hole in one back leg. Hal stuck his fingers in the hole. He pulled out some cotton. "It's falling apart," he said.

"Mrs. Walker," Chuck called, "can we have this elephant?"

"All right," she said. "But if your mom won't let you keep it, bring it back here."

Chuck picked up the front of the elephant. Hal picked up the back. It wasn't too heavy at first.

Mrs. Walker gave them a dollar. "Thanks for the help, boys."

"Just a minute," Hal said. "I have to get my other stuff."

"Leave that junk," Chuck said.

Hal left the tire and the airplane. But he shoved the yo-yo into his pocket.

They carried the elephant down the street. It got heavy in a hurry. "This is the greatest idea I ever had," Chuck said. "We'll sell this thing for a bunch of money. We won't have to work any more."

"Let's sell it fast," Hal said. "My arms hurt."

"We'll sell it to Mrs. Baker," Chuck said. "Brandon and the baby will love it."

They carried the elephant two blocks

to Mrs. Baker's house. They stopped and rested nine times.

Hal lay down on Mrs. Baker's lawn. He was too hot and tired to go any farther. He watched Chuck ring the bell.

Mrs. Baker came to the door. She just had Brandon with her. "Hi, Mrs. Baker," Chuck said. "We found something Brandon might like."

"Oh," Mrs. Baker said. She didn't sound very happy.

"Come look at it, Brandon," Chuck said. "Isn't it neat?"

"Nooo," Brandon said.

"Come and give it a pat," Chuck said.

"Nooo," Brandon said, louder than before.

"We'd better go in before he wakes the baby," Mrs. Baker said. She closed the door.

Chuck dragged the elephant back to the sidewalk. Hal stayed on the lawn. "I can't move," he said.

"I see something down the street," Chuck said.

"I don't care," Hal said. "I can't move."

"It looks like a lemonade stand," Chuck said. "In front of Rick's house."

Hal sat up. "Maybe I can move a little."

Chapter 4

Hal and Chuck carried the pink elephant down the street. Sally, Rick's little sister, was sitting in a lawn chair.

"Lemonade for sale," she called to them.

The sign on the stand said
LEMONADE 35¢.

"We'll take two cups," Chuck said. They set down the elephant.

A window in the house opened. "Don't buy her stupid lemonade," Rick yelled. "It might be poison."

"He's just mad," Sally said. "He has to stay in his room for an hour."

"What did he do?" Hal asked.

Sally filled two cups. "He asked for a cup of lemonade and drank it. Then he said he didn't have any money. He thought it was a big joke."

Hal reached for a cup. But Sally pushed away his hand. "From now on, I get the money first."

Chuck gave her the dollar from Mrs. Walker. Then he and Hal grabbed the cups and drank.

"I don't have any change," Sally said.

Chuck set down his empty cup. "Then give me back the dollar. I'll pay you later."

Sally held the dollar behind her back. "I'll give you the change later."

"I hope the lemonade makes you sick," Rick yelled. He banged the window shut.

Hal looked at his empty cup. "Can I have a little more?"

"Do you have some more money?" Sally asked.

"Give us another cup," Chuck said. "Then you can keep the change."

Sally filled their cups. "Are you going to the magic show with us?" she asked.

"I don't know," Hal said. "We have to earn the money."

"We're going," Chuck said.

Hal looked at the lemonade stand. Maybe he and Chuck could put up a

stand like that. It would be easier to sell lemonade than an elephant.

"Sally," he said, "is it fun to have a lemonade stand?"

"It's great," Sally said.

Hal smiled. "How much money have you made?"

"Let's see," Sally said. "So far I've made a dollar."

Hal shook his head. Maybe it wasn't such a good idea after all.

"Sally," Chuck said, "what do you think of this elephant? Isn't it neat?"

"It's dirty," Sally said.

"It's for sale," Chuck said. "Maybe your mom could buy it for you."

"It smells bad," Sally said. "And it has a hole in its leg."

"Only six dollars," Chuck said.

"You can have it for one dollar," Hal whispered. He didn't want to carry it any more.

Sally shook her head. "I don't want it."

"Would you trade for one more cup of lemonade?" Hal asked.

Sally put her fingers in her ears and shouted, "I don't want that old thing."

"You'll be sorry," Chuck said.

But Sally just shook her head and kept her fingers in her ears.

Hal and Chuck carried the elephant up the street. "Now what?" Hal asked.

"I'm thinking," Chuck said.

"I'm dying," Hal said.

"We can try some more houses," Chuck said.

Hal looked at the elephant. One of

its ears was coming off. "We can't sell this thing."

"Then let's get rid of it," Chuck said.

"How?"

"Just watch me," Chuck said. "The Amazing Chuck will make this thing disappear."

Up the street two girls were playing hopscotch on the sidewalk. "Look what we have," Chuck said.

"You're in our way," one girl said.

"This is Fred," Chuck said. "Don't you want to pat Fred?"

"Don't touch him," the girl told her friend. "He's dirty. He probably has cooties." Both girls giggled.

Hal and Chuck picked up the elephant and walked on. "Bye-bye, Fred," one girl called.

Hal and Chuck carried the elephant back to Mrs. Walker's house. They rested twelve times on the way.

The trash man hadn't come yet. Hal picked up the airplane and the tire. Then he put them back. He was too tired to carry anything.

"It's getting late," Hal said. "We'd better go home and pull weeds for Dad."

"Okay," Chuck said. "If that's what you want to do."

They walked home slowly. Dad was in the front yard. He was pulling weeds. Hal started to run. "Dad," he called, "don't pull all the weeds. Save some for us."

Dad looked up and smiled. "Don't worry. We have plenty for everybody."

Pulling weeds was hard work. Hal got tired. And his arms itched. But at least he didn't have to look cute.

Part Two:
The Amazing Victor

Chapter 5

Hal went to the magic show with Chuck, Rick, and Sally. "Let's sit in the front row," Hal said. "I want to see everything."

They found four seats right in front. "Maybe this is too close," Sally said. "The Amazing Victor might turn us into frogs."

"You'd look better that way," Rick said.

"Magic like that is only in stories," Hal told her.

"Yeah," Chuck said. "This stuff is just tricks. Anybody can do them."

"Really?" Sally said.

"Sure," Chuck said. "I've read lots of magic books. I know how to do all kinds of tricks."

"Does he?" Sally asked Hal.

"Chuck knows everything," Hal said. "Just ask him."

"Do you know how to saw somebody in half?" Sally asked.

"I'll saw you in half," Rick said.

"That's easy," Chuck said. "You get two little guys in the box. One sticks his head out. One sticks out his feet."

"It's not that easy," Hal said. "When I saw it on TV, a girl got into an empty box. And her head and feet were sticking out before they closed the lid."

"The show is starting," Chuck said.

The lights got dim. The stage lights came on. "Ladies and gentlemen," a voice said, "here he is—The Amazing Victor."

Hal and Sally clapped. The Amazing Victor walked onstage and took a bow. He held out a vase of flowers. Then he put a black cloth over them. He waved his wand and took off the cloth. Instead of flowers, he had two white birds.

"Wow," Hal said.

"He had the birds in his sleeve," Chuck said.

Victor put the cloth over the birds. He waved the wand and took off the

cloth. The birds were still there. But now they were inside a big cage.

"Where did the cage come from?" Hal whispered. "Was it up his sleeve too?"

"Quiet," Chuck said. "I want to watch the show."

The Amazing Victor brought out a table. The tablecloth went to the floor. "He hides stuff behind that cloth," Chuck said.

Victor did tricks with rings. He did tricks with balls. He pulled a rabbit out of his hat. "That's an easy one," Chuck said.

Hal loved all the tricks. He wished he could do magic. Maybe he could get a book and learn how. Maybe he could become The Amazing Hal.

Victor pushed a big red box onto the stage. The box came up to Victor's chin. On the front of the box were two doors. "This is my magic box," Victor said. He came to the edge of the stage. "I need two boys to help me. But I'd better warn you. I'm going to make the boys disappear. So, Moms and Dads, if you like your boys, don't send them up here. They might not come back."

Everybody laughed.

"Now," said Victor, "who wants to help me?"

Chuck and Rick raised their hands right away. Hal didn't know if he should put up his hand or not.

"Why do boys get all the fun?" Sally said.

Hal put up his hand. But not too high.

Chuck and Rick were waving their hands in the air. "Here are two boys who want to disappear," The Amazing Victor said. "Come up here."

Chuck and Rick ran up the steps to the stage. Hal wished he could go too. Sort of.

"Give these boys a hand," Victor said. A few people clapped. Chuck took a bow. Rick waved.

"Now, boys," said Victor, "you're sure it's okay if you disappear?"

"No problem," Chuck said.

"It's okay," Rick said. He didn't sound as sure as Chuck.

Victor opened the doors of the

magic box. "Step right in, boys."

Chuck went in the first door. He could barely fit inside. Rick went in the second door. Victor closed it.

Victor waved his wand. Then he opened the doors. Chuck and Rick were standing there. "You guys still here?"

Victor closed the doors again. Then he waved his wand harder. "Now let's try it." He threw open the doors.

Nobody was there.

"Where'd they go?" Hal whispered.

Victor closed the doors again. "Getting rid of them is easy," he said. "The hard part is bringing them back."

He waved his wand. Then he looked out at the people. "I don't know. Do you miss those guys?"

Hal thought about it. No, he didn't miss Chuck. Not much, anyway.

Victor opened a door. There was Rick.

"How'd he do that?" Hal asked.

Victor closed the door. He moved to the other door. "Who do you think is here?" he asked.

"Chuck," Hal shouted.

Victor opened the door. Chuck wasn't there. It was Rick again.

Everybody laughed.

Victor scratched his head. "You look like somebody I know," he said. He closed the door and opened the other one. Rick was there too.

Where was Chuck? Hal wondered.

"Come out here, son," Victor said to

Rick. Rick came out and waved to the audience.

"This is neat," Sally whispered.

"Where's your pal?" Victor asked Rick.

"I don't know," Rick said.

"Is he in here?" Victor asked. He threw open both doors. Nobody was in the box.

Everybody clapped.

"Chuck must be behind the box," Hal whispered.

"Don't worry," Victor told Rick. "We'll find him. Even if we have to take the place apart."

Victor took the doors off the box. He set them down flat on the stage. Then he took down one side of the box. Then another side.

Only the back of the box was left standing. Victor smiled at the audience. "You know where he is?"

"Yes," some people yelled.

Victor shook his head. "I don't think so." He took down the back.

Chuck wasn't there.

Hal began to worry.

"I think I heard something," Victor said. He reached under a door and brought out a bird. He gave it to Rick. He reached under the other door and found flowers. He gave those to Rick. Victor found a hat. And more birds. And even the birdcage. Rick carried everything offstage.

"Where's Chuck?" Hal whispered to Sally.

"Don't worry," she said. "It's just a trick."

Victor came to the edge of the stage. "Well, I warned you," he said. He looked down at Sally. "Was he your brother?"

"No, he was *his* brother." Sally pointed at Hal.

"Stand up," Victor said. Hal stood up. "Tell us. What kind of brother was he?"

"Okay," Hal said. Chuck *was* okay sometimes.

Victor laughed. "Okay, huh? Not too good. Just okay?" He stepped back. "That's good. You won't miss him too much then. If you want him back, come to my show next year. I'll see what I can do."

Everybody laughed. Everybody but Hal. He slid back into his seat. Sally was right. It was a trick. Chuck wasn't really gone. But Hal still wished Chuck would show up.

Victor did some more tricks. Hal kept waiting for Chuck to come back.

The curtain came down. The show was over. Victor came out to take a bow.

He bowed three times. Then he picked up the table. There was Chuck—sitting under it. Everybody laughed and clapped. Especially Hal.

"What's this?" Victor said. He set down the table. The tablecloth hid Chuck again. "I need this guy for next year's show."

Victor waved his wand. Then he lifted the table again. Chuck wasn't there any more. Victor bowed and walked offstage with the table. The tablecloth dragged on the floor.

"Chuck's still under the table," Hal whispered. Sally nodded.

Just then Victor stopped and pulled the cloth off the table. There was nobody there. Victor bowed and went behind the curtain.

"Don't worry," Sally said. "Chuck's not really gone."

"I know that," Hal said. But he'd feel better when he saw Chuck again.

Chapter 6

The lights came on. Sally jumped up from her chair. "Wait right here," she said.

"Where are you going?" Hal asked.

"Never mind," she said. "Just wait here."

"I want to know where you're going."

"It's none of your business," Sally said. "But I have to go to the rest room. Bad. So wait right here." She ran up the aisle.

Hal looked around. It had been a great show. But he wished Chuck would come back.

Rick came out from behind the curtain. He looked worried.

"What's the matter?" Hal asked.

"I don't want to scare you," Rick said. "But Chuck's gone."

Hal stared at him. "What do you mean?"

"He's not back there," Rick said. "He's not anywhere. The Amazing Victor made him disappear."

"No way," Hal said.

"I didn't believe it myself," Rick said in a shaky voice. "But it's true. Chuck is gone." Rick had tears in his eyes.

Hal looked at the stage. He didn't

believe Rick. But he couldn't be sure.

"Where's Sally?" Rick asked.

"She had to go to the rest room," Hal said.

"She always does," Rick said. "When she comes back, come up onstage. Maybe I can fix things."

"What do you mean?" Hal asked.

"I was watching The Amazing Victor," Rick said. "I think I know how to do the trick. Maybe I can bring Chuck back myself." He went up the steps.

Hal looked at the side door. He hoped Sally would hurry.

Sally came back a few minutes later. "What took you so long?" Hal asked.

"There was a big line," Sally said.

"There's always a big line when I'm in a hurry."

"Rick said for us to go up onstage," Hal told her. "Something's wrong. The Amazing Victor didn't bring Chuck back."

Sally shook her head. "Don't listen to Rick. He's just trying to scare us."

"That's what I thought," Hal said. "But he looked worried. And he even had tears in his eyes."

"It's a big fake," Sally said. "He does that all the time. He and Chuck are playing a trick."

Hal looked at the stage. "That's mean."

"Let's go tell my dad," Sally said.

Hal smiled. "No, we don't want to

tell. Let's play our own trick."

Sally jumped up and down. "Goody-goody." It didn't sound dumb when she said it.

"We have to look sad," Hal told her. "And scared."

Sally looked sad for a second. Then she giggled.

"Come on," Hal said. "No laughing."

They put on sad looks. Then they went up the steps to the stage.

Rick came over to them. "It's about time you got here."

"Did The Amazing Victor bring Chuck back?" Hal asked.

Rick shook his head. "He won't do it."

"What can I tell Mom and Dad?" Hal said.

Sally started to giggle. Hal poked her. She put her hand over her mouth.

"I'm scared," Rick said. "I hope Chuck's all right."

"Maybe we should call the police," Hal said.

Sally held both hands over her mouth. Her whole body was shaking. Hal hoped she didn't laugh out loud.

"Maybe I can help," Rick said. "Come back here." He took them to the back of the stage. He stopped next to a white curtain. Hal could see sneakers sticking out from under it.

"I think I can do the trick," Rick said. "I think I can bring Chuck back."

He put his hands over his eyes. "Be very quiet."

"Wait a minute," Hal said. "I'm not sure I want you to bring Chuck back."

Rick turned and looked at Hal. "What?"

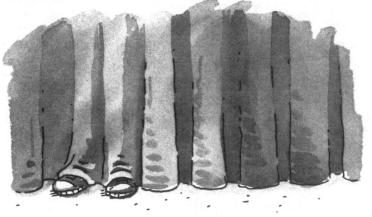

"Let me think about it for a minute," Hal said. "If Chuck doesn't come back, then I get his train and his baseball bat."

Hal saw the curtain wiggle.

"Don't be stupid," Rick said. "I'll do the trick and bring him back."

"I don't think so," Hal said. "Let's just forget it."

The curtain wiggled some more.

"We've got to get him back," Rick said. "What would your mom and dad say?"

"I don't think they'd miss him much," Hal said. "He was a pain most of the time."

Chuck yanked back the curtain. "I heard that," he yelled.

Sally dropped her hands and laughed out loud.

"See?" Hal said to her. "I brought Chuck back all by myself. You can call me The Amazing Hal."

Sally and Hal laughed all the way home.

"It wasn't that funny," Chuck said.

But that made them laugh even more.

Part Three:
The Amazing Hal

Chapter 7

The day after the magic show Hal went to the library. He checked out two magic books. The next day he checked out two more.

On his way home he saw Sally at her lemonade stand. "I'm learning magic," he told her. "Pretty soon The Amazing Hal will have a magic show."

"Will it be free?" Sally asked.

"I don't know," Hal said. He hadn't thought about money.

"I hope it's free," Sally said. "I'm broke. I'm not making any money with this stand."

"What's the matter?" Hal asked.

"Nobody has any money," Sally said. "They give it all to the ice cream man. So nobody buys my lemonade. And I get hot and drink it all."

Hal looked at the pitcher. "I like lemonade."

"But you don't have any money. Right?"

"Right," Hal said. "But I'll let you come to my show for free."

Sally poured him a cup of lemonade. "It better be a good show."

Hal drank his lemonade. He loved magic. He'd already gotten free lemonade, and he hadn't learned one trick yet.

One book had tricks Hal could do. And it showed how to make a magician's hat out of an oatmeal box and a paper plate.

Hal made a good hat. But it had to be painted. Hal didn't have any black paint. So he used black shoe polish. The shoe polish made the hat black. But it came off on his fingers. And his face. And his clothes.

Mom made him throw away that hat.

He made another hat out of black poster paper. That worked better. And he used a black pencil for a wand.

Now he was ready to give a show. But it was hard to learn tricks. "Chuck," he asked, "how many tricks do I need for a show?"

"For a good show, you need fifty," Chuck said. "For a so-so show, you need twenty-five. How many do you have?"

"I don't know," Hal said.

But he did know. He had two.

A few days later Hal asked Mom, "How many tricks do I need for a magic show?"

"How many do you have?" she asked.

"Three," Hal said.

Mom smiled. "That's sounds just right."

Hal went down the street to Sally's house. "Come to the magic show," he told her. "Come see The Amazing Hal."

Sally jumped up and down. "Goody-goody," she shouted.

"Rick can come too," Hal said.

"Are you sure you want him?" Sally asked.

"Sure," Hal said. "It'll be a good show."

Hal and Sally ran back to Hal's house. Rick came too. But he didn't run.

Hal ran into the living room. Mom and Dad were reading the newspaper. Chuck was watching cartoons on TV. "Come to the magic show in my bedroom," Hal said. "Come see The Amazing Hal."

"Great," Dad said.

"This will be fun," Mom said.

"This will be dumb," Chuck said.

Sally and Mom sat on chairs. Dad sat on Hal's bed. Chuck and Rick sat on the floor.

Hal went out into the hall. He put on his black hat and waved his wand. Then he shouted, "Here he is—The Amazing Hal."

Hal came into the bedroom. Everybody clapped but Chuck. Hal took a bow, and his hat fell off. Rick and Chuck laughed.

Hal put on his hat and handed Mom a box of crayons. "This is the amazing crayon trick," he said. "When I turn my back, take them all out but one. Then close the box." He turned his back.

"What are you going to do?" Sally asked.

"I'll tell you which crayon is left in the box," Hal said.

"Hide the rest of the crayons," Chuck said.

In a minute Mom said, "Ready."

Hal turned around and took the box. He held it behind his back. "I'm thinking," he said. "I'm thinking." Then he brought out one hand and banged the table. "Red!" he shouted. He opened the box and showed them the red crayon.

"Wow!" Sally said.

"That's wonderful," Mom said.

"That's amazing," Dad said.

"I know how you did that," Chuck said. "You reached into the box and got some crayon on your thumbnail. Then you looked at your thumbnail when you hit the table."

Chuck and Rick laughed.

Hal wanted to stick out his tongue. But he didn't. The Amazing Hal didn't do things like that.

Next Hal put ten pennies on the table. He told Sally to take a pencil and mark one. Then Hal put all ten pennies in a paper bag. "The one you marked will be heavier because of the lead on it," he said. He reached into the sack

without looking and felt around. "This one seems heavier. Much heavier." He brought out a penny and gave it to Sally.

"That's my penny!" Sally shouted. "Look. There's my mark."

"That's wonderful," Mom said.

"Amazing," Dad said.

"I know how you did that," Chuck said.

"That's enough, Chuck," Dad said.

But Chuck whispered, "You put a little piece of gum on that one when you put it in the bag."

He and Rick laughed.

Hal went on with the show. It was time for his big trick. He had worked on it for a week. Even Chuck wouldn't guess this one.

He looked at his watch and shook his head. "My watch never works right." He took off the watch and held it in his fist. Then, with his other hand, he pretended to take a gun from his pocket. He pointed his finger at his closed fist and said, "Bang." Then he smiled and said, "That's one way to kill time."

Everyone laughed but Chuck.

"Look out," Hal said. "You know how time flies when you're having fun." He opened his fist. The watch was gone.

"Oh, wow!" Sally said.

"Wonderful," Mom said.

"Amazing," Dad said.

"I know how you did that," Chuck said.

"Chuck!" Dad said.

"You had a rubber band hooked onto the watch," Chuck yelled out. "The watch went up your sleeve. I saw it."

Chuck laughed and laughed. So did Rick.

"The show's over," Hal said. He took off his hat and sat down on the floor.

"Hey, Amazing Hal," Chuck said, "let me know when you have your next show. Rick and I can always use a good laugh." He and Rick went back to the living room.

"Big brothers are a big pain," Sally said to Hal.

"That was a good show," Dad said. "We all liked it."

"Not Chuck," Hal said.

"Chuck loved it," Dad said.

"I'm no good at magic," Hal said.

"You're great at magic," Mom said. "You made us all happy. And that's the best magic of all."

But right then The Amazing Hal didn't want to make people happy. He wanted to trick them. Especially his rotten big brother Chuck.

Chapter 8

Hal and Sally sat on the lawn. "It's not fair," Hal said. "Chuck read all the magic books."

"Big brothers are mean," Sally said.

Mrs. Brown was sweeping her sidewalk. "Hi there," she called. "Why do you look so sad?"

"I'm not sad," Hal said. "I'm mad."

"Hal just gave a neat magic show," Sally said. "But Chuck told how he did all the tricks."

"A magic show?" Mrs. Brown said.

"And I didn't get to come?"

"You didn't miss much," Hal said.

"Didn't everybody have fun?" Mrs. Brown asked.

"I did," Sally said.

"I didn't have fun," Hal said.

"I haven't seen a magic show in years," Mrs. Brown said. "Could you put on a magic show for me?"

"I don't know," Hal said. "I think I'm done with magic shows."

"I just made some cookies," Mrs. Brown told him. "Oatmeal raisin."

Hal stood up. "I guess we could have a show."

"I'll get some lemonade," Sally said.

The Amazing Hal put on a show for

Sally and Mrs. Brown and Buster, Mrs. Brown's cat. Everybody liked the show. And nobody guessed the tricks.

After the show they ate oatmeal raisin cookies and drank lemonade.

"That was fun," Mrs. Brown said. "You *are* amazing."

"I'm not amazing enough," Hal said. "Chuck guessed all my tricks."

"Chuck is a pain," Sally said. "Just like Rick."

"I wish I could do a trick to fool Chuck," Hal said.

"Maybe you could saw somebody in half," Sally said.

Hal shook his head. "I don't know how. And I don't even have a saw."

"Have another cookie," Mrs. Brown

said. "Maybe if we all work together, we can think of a trick to fool Chuck."

Later that day Hal and Sally came into the living room. Chuck and Rick were watching TV. Hal had on his black hat. He had his wand in his hand. "Come to the bedroom," he said. "The Amazing Hal has one more trick."

"Great," Dad said.

"Wonderful," Mom said.

"Big deal," Chuck said.

Rick laughed.

They all went into the bedroom. Sally stood by the wall. "Here he is," she shouted. "The Amazing Hal."

Mom and Dad clapped. "Big deal,"

Chuck said. Rick laughed.

Hal came in and took a bow. This time he took off his hat first.

Hal held up a basket. "This is Amazing Hal's amazing basket." He let them look at it.

"That's Mom's old fruit basket," Chuck said.

"It's a magic basket," Hal said. He put a red cloth in the basket. Then he set the basket on the table by the window.

"There's something in the cloth," Chuck said.

"No, there isn't," Sally said.

"You'd better check," Hal told him.

Chuck lifted up the cloth. "Nothing there."

Sally smiled. "See?"

"Just wait," Hal said. He waved his magic wand three times.

Chuck laughed. "Nothing happened."

"I'm not done," Hal said. "This is a hard trick." He waved his wand again. "We have to go to the living room for the next part."

Hal led them into the living room. He waved his wand. "I can feel magic in the air," he said.

"This is dumb," Chuck said.

"Really dumb," Rick said.

Sally looked at Hal and smiled.

"Now we have to go into the kitchen," Hal said.

In the kitchen Hal waved his wand. "The magic is working," he said. He waved the wand over the counter. "It's fixing something good for us." He waved his wand by the oven. "Now it's baking something for us."

"This is so dumb," Chuck said.

"Yeah," Rick said.

"We'll see," Sally said.

Hal waved his wand one more time. "Now it's sending the surprise through the air." He led them back to his bedroom. He opened the door and let the others go in first.

"There's something in the basket," Mom said.

Chuck ran over and lifted up the cloth. The basket was full of cookies.

"That's a great trick," Mom said.

"Amazing," said Dad.

"Have a cookie," Hal said.

Sally took a cookie. "Oatmeal raisin," she said. "My favorite kind."

Chuck looked at Rick.

"I don't get it," Rick said.

Hal laughed and laughed.

"How did you do it?" Chuck asked.

Hal laughed. "It was magic," he said.

"Tell me," Chuck begged.

"Maybe later."

"Please," Chuck said. "I'll buy you an ice cream bar."

"I'll think about it," Hal said.

He didn't tell Chuck for a whole week.

It was a very good week for Hal.